To:

From:

LITTLE SIMON
An imprint of Simon & Schuster Children's Publishing Division
1230 Avenue of the Americas, New York, New York 10020
Text copyright © 2001 by Simon & Schuster
Other text derived from American Greetings cards © 2001 AGC, Inc.
Bubblegum™, Bubblegum Logo™, and character designs © 2001 AGC, Inc., used under license.
All rights reserved including the right of reproduction in whole or in part in any form.
LITTLE SIMON and colophon are registered trademarks of Simon & Schuster.
Manufactured in China
First Edition
2 4 6 8 10 9 7 5 3 1
ISBN 0-689-84705-X

Cool Christmas Cheer

Bubblegum

LITTLE SIMON

New York   London   Toronto   Sydney   Singapore

Break out the tinsel and the star.

Christmastime is here!

Put up the lights and trim the tree,

And deck the halls with cheer!

Getting gifts can be groovy,

But giving them is more fun.

Buy it, make it, or do something fab.

It doesn't matter which one!

Santa has you on his list.

So what should be your goal?

Be nice—'cause if you're naughty,

All you'll get is coal!

Stand beneath the mistletoe

And you will get a smooch.

They say it works for everyone—

Even for a pooch!

Winter means cold weather
And ice and sleet and snow.
Chill out, but don't you freeze—
Suit up from head to toe!

It's the season to come back home,

Whether far off or near.

So hit the road, pick up the pace,

By plane, or skis, or deer!

I haven't kept in touch,

But there's one thing I must say,

Have the coolest yuletide ever—

A jolly holiday!

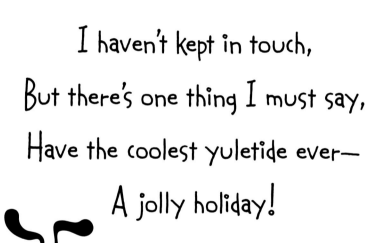

Vacation's here at last!

Let's party and let's play—

Right now before the snow

Completely melts away.

Christmas cheer and understanding

Is what you always lend.

You're a little ray of fabness,

My bestest-ever friend!

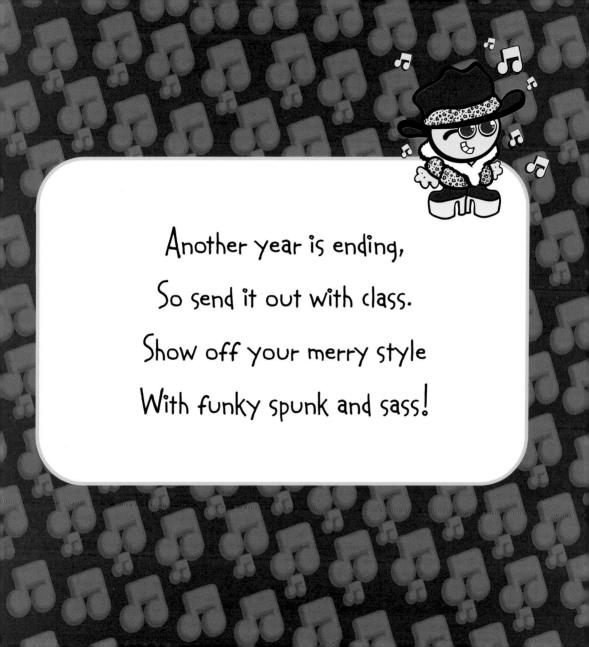

Another year is ending,

So send it out with class.

Show off your merry style

With funky spunk and sass!

Spending time together

Makes holidays complete.

We're one terrific team

That simply can't be beat!

Keep Christmas in your heart
Each day the whole year through.
Then cool yule love will show itself
In everything you do!